Mrs. Pendleton's F

Gertrude Franklin Horn Atherton

Alpha Editions

This edition published in 2023

ISBN : 9789357954853

Design and Setting By
Alpha Editions
www.alphaedis.com
Email - info@alphaedis.com

Contents

I

Jessica, her hands clenched and teeth set, stood looking with hard eyes at a small heap of letters lying on the floor. The sun, blazing through the open window, made her blink unconsciously, and the ocean's deep voice rising to the Newport sands seemed to reiterate:—

"Contempt! Contempt!"

Tall, finely pointed with the indescribable air and style of the New York woman, she did not suggest intimate knowledge of the word the ocean hurled to her. In that moss-green room, with her haughty face and clean skin, her severe faultless gown, she rather suggested the type to whom poets a century hence would indite their sonnets—when she and her kind had been set in the frame of the past. And if her dress was conventional, she had let imagination play with her hair. The clear evasive colour of flame, it was brushed down to her neck, parted, crossed, and brought tightly up each side of her head just behind her ears. Meeting above her bang, the curling ends allowed to fly loose, it vaguely resembled Medusa's wreath. Her eyes were grey, the colour of mid-ocean, calm, beneath a grey sky. Not twenty-four, she had the repose and "air" of one whose cradle had been rocked by Society's foot; and although at this moment her pride was in the dust, there was more anger than shame in her face.

The door opened and her hostess entered. As Mrs. Pendleton turned slowly and looked at her, Miss Decker gave a little cry.

"'I HAVE BEEN INSULTED.'"

"Jessica!" she said, "what is the matter?"

"I have been insulted," said Mrs. Pendleton, deliberately. She felt a savage pleasure in further humiliating herself.

"Insulted! You!" Miss Decker's correct voice and calm brown eyes could not have expressed more surprise and horror if a foreign diplomatist had snapped his fingers in the face of the President's wife. Even her sleek brown hair almost quivered.

"Yes," Mrs. Pendleton went on in the same measured tones; "four men have told me how much they despise me." She walked slowly up and down the room. Miss Decker sank upon the divan, incredulity, curiosity, expectation, feminine satisfaction marching across her face in rapid procession.

"I have always maintained that a married woman has a perfect right to flirt," continued Mrs. Pendleton. "The more if she has married an old man and life is somewhat of a bore. 'Why do you marry an old man?' snaps the virtuous world. 'What a contemptible creature you are to marry for anything but love!' it cries, as it eats the dust at Mammon's feet. I married an old man because with the wisdom of twenty, I had made up my mind that I could never love and that position and wealth alone made up the sum of existence. I had more excuse than a girl who has been always poor, for I had never known the arithmetic of money until my father failed, the year before I married. People who have never known wealth do not realise the purely physical suffering of those inured to luxury and suddenly bereft of it: it makes no difference what one's will or strength of character is. So—I married Mr. Pendleton. So—I amused myself with other men. Mr. Pendleton gave me my head, because I kept clear of scandal: he knew my pride. Now, if I had spent my life demoralising myself and the society that received me, I could not be more bitterly punished. I suppose I deserve it. I suppose that the married flirt is just as poor and paltry and contemptible a creature as the moralist and the minister depict her. We measure morals by results. Therefore I hold to-day that it is the business of a lifetime to throw stones at the married flirt."

"For Heaven's sake," cried Miss Decker, in a tone of exasperation, "stop moralising and tell me what has happened!"

"Do you remember Clarence Trent, Edward Dedham, John Severance, Norton Boswell?"

"Do I? Poor moths!"

"They were apparently devoted to me."

Dryly: "Apparently."

"How long is it since Mr. Pendleton's death?"

"About—he died on the sixteenth—why, yes, it was six months yesterday since he died."

"Exactly. You see these four notes on the floor? They are four proposals—four proposals"—and she gave a short hard laugh through lips whose red had suddenly faded—"from the four men I have just mentioned."

Miss Decker gasped. "Four proposals! Then what on earth are you angry about?"

Mrs. Pendleton's lip curled scornfully. She did not condescend to answer at once. "You are clever enough at times," she said coldly, after a moment. "It is odd you cannot grasp the very palpable fact that four proposals received on the same day, by the same mail, from four men who are each other's most intimate friends, can mean but one thing—a practical joke. Oh!" she cried, the jealously mastered passion springing into her voice, "that is what infuriates me—more even than the insult—that they should think me such a fool as to be so easily deceived! O—h—h!"

"If I remember aright," ventured Miss Decker, feebly, "the intimacy to which you allude was a thing of the past some time before you disappeared from the world. In fact, they were not on speaking terms."

"Oh, they have made it up long ago! Don't make any weak explanations, but tell me how to turn the tables on them. I would give my hair and wear a grey wig—my complexion and paint—to get even with them. And I will. But how? How?"

She paced up and down the room with nervous steps, glancing for inspiration from the delicate etchings on the walls to the divan that was like a moss bank, to the carpet that might have been a patch of forest green, and thence to the sparkling ocean. Miss Decker offered no suggestions. She had perfect faith in the genius of her friend.

Suddenly Mrs. Pendleton paused and turned to her hostess. The red had come back to her curled mouth. Her eyes were luminous, as when the sun breaks through the grey sky and falls, dazzling, on the waters.

"I have it!" she said. "And a week from to-day—I will keep them in suspense that long—New York will have no corner small enough to hold them."

II

The hot September day was ten hours old. The office of the St. Christopher Club was still deserted but for a clerk who looked warm and sleepy. The postman had just left a heap of letters on his desk, and he was sorting them for their various pigeonholes. A young man entered, and the clerk began to turn over the letters more rapidly. The newcomer, tall, thin, with sharp features and shrewd American face, had an extremely nervous manner. As he passed through the vestibule a clerk at a table put a mark opposite the name "Mr. Clarence Trent," to indicate that he was in the Club.

"Any letters?" he demanded of the office clerk.

The man handed him two, and he darted into the morning-room and tore one open, letting the other fall to the floor. He read as follows:—

> "Mon ami!—I have but this moment received your letter, which seems to have been delayed. ["Of course! Why did I not think of that?"] I say nothing here of the happiness which its contents have given me. Come at once.
> > "Jessica Pendleton.
>
> "Our engagement must be a profound secret until the year of my mourning is over."

Trent's drab and scanty whiskers seemed to curl into hard knots over the nervous facial contortion in which he indulged. Nature being out of material when at work upon him had seemingly constructed his muscles from stout twine. An inch of it joining his nose to the upper lip, the former's pointed tip was wont to punctuate his conversation and emotions with the direct downward movement of a machine needle puncturing cloth. He crumpled the letter in his bony nervous fingers, and his pale sharp grey eyes opened and shut with sudden rapidity.

"I knew I could not be mistaken," he thought triumphantly. "She is mine!"

In the vestibule another name was checked off,—"Mr. Norton Boswell,"—and its owner made eagerly for the desk. His dark intellectual face was flushed, and his sensitive mouth twitched suddenly as the clerk handed him a roll of Mss.

"Never mind that," he said hastily. "Give me my letters."

The clerk handed him several, and, whisking them from left to right through his impatient hands, he thrust all but one into his pocket and walked rapidly to the morning-room. Seating himself before a table, he looked at the envelope as if not daring to solve its mystery, then hastily tore it apart.

"Mon ami! [Boswell, despite his ardour, threw a glance down a certain corridor in his memory and thought with kindling eyes: "Oh! with what divine sweetness did she use to utter those two little words!" Then he fixed his eyes greedily on the page once more.] I have but this moment received your letter, which seems to have been delayed." ["Ah!" rapturously, the paper dancing before his eyes, "that accounts for it. I knew she was the most tender-hearted creature on earth."] "I say nothing here of the happiness which its contents have given me. Come at once.

"Jessica Pendleton.

"Our engagement must be a profound secret until the year of my mourning is over."

Boswell, with quivering nostrils, plunged a pen into the ink-well, and in that quiet room two hearts thumped so loudly that only passion and scratching pens averted mutual and withering contempt.

As Boswell left the office a very young man entered it. He possessed that nondescript blond complexion which seems to be the uniform of the New York youth of fashion. The ciphers of the Four Hundred have achieved the well-scrubbed appearance of the Anglo-Saxon more successfully than his accent. Mr. Dedham might have been put through a clothes-wringer. Even his minute and recent moustache looked as if each hair had its particular nurse, and his pink and chubby face defied conscientious dissipation. He sauntered up to the clerk's desk with an elaborate affectation of indifference, and drawled a demand for his mail.

The clerk handed him a dainty note sealed with a crest. He accepted it with an absent air, although a look of genuine boyish delight thrust its way through the fishy inertness of his average expression.

It took him a minute and a half to get into the morning-room and read these fateful lines:—

"Mon ami,—["Enchanting phrase! I can hear her say it."] I have but this moment received your letter, which seems to have been delayed. ["Ah! this perfume! this perfume!"] I say nothing here of the happiness which its contents have given me. Come at once.

"Jessica Pendleton.

"Our engagement must be a profound secret until the year of my mourning is over."

A rosy tide wandered to the roots of Mr. Dedham's ashen locks, and he made a wild uncertain dab at his upper lip. Again there was no sound in the morning-room of the St. Christopher Club but the furious dashing of pens, the rending of parchment paper, the sudden scraping of a nervous foot.

A tall broad-shouldered young man, with much repose of face and manner, entered the office from the avenue, glanced at the pigeon-holes above the clerk's desk, then sauntered deliberately into the morning-room and looked out of the window. A slight rigidity of the nostrils alone betokened the impatience within, and his uneasy thoughts ran somewhat as follows:—

"What a fool I have been! After all my experience with women to make such an ass of myself over the veriest coquette that ever breathed; but her preference for me last winter was so pointed—oh, damnation!"

He stood gnawing his underlip at the lumbering 'bus, but turned suddenly as a man approached from behind and presented several letters on a tray. The first and only one he opened ran thus:—

> "Mon ami!—I have but this moment received your letter, which seems to have been delayed. I say nothing here of the happiness which its contents have given me. Come at once.
>   "Jessica Pendleton.

> "Our engagement must be a profound secret until the year of my mourning is over."

Severance folded the note, his face paling a little.

"Well, well, she is true after all. What a brute I was to misjudge her!" He strolled back to the office. "I will go home and write to her, and to-morrow I shall see her! Great Heaven! Were six months ever so long before?"

As he turned from the coat-room Boswell entered the office by the opposite door.

"The fellow looks as gay as a lark," he thought. "He hasn't looked like that for six months. I believe I'll make it up with him—particularly as I've come out ahead!"

"Give me that package," demanded Boswell dreamily of the clerk. Then he caught sight of Severance. "Why, Jack, old fellow!" he cried, "how are you? Haven't seen you looking so well for an age. Don't go out. It's too hot."

"Oh, hang it! I've got to. I'm off for Newport to-morrow. It's so infernally dull in town."

"Going to Newport to-morrow! So am I. My aunt is quite ill and has sent for me. I'm her heir, you know."

"No? Didn't know you had an aunt. I congratulate you. Hope she'll go off, I'm sure."

"Hope so. Here comes Teddy,—looks like an elongated rubber ball. It's some time since I've seen him so buoyant. How are you, Teddy?"

"How are you, Norton, old boy?" explained Dedham, rapturously. "How glad I am to hear the old name once more! You've given me the cold shoulder of late."

"Oh, well, my boy, you know men will be fools occasionally. But give by-gones the go-by. I'm going to Newport to-morrow. Can I take any messages to your numerous—"

"Dear boy! I'm going to Newport to-morrow. Sea-bathing ordered by my physician."

"Jove! I am in luck! Severance is going over, too. We'll have a jolly time of it."

"I should say so!" murmured Teddy. "Heaven! Hello, Sev, how are you? Didn't see you. As long as we are all going the same way we might as well bury our hatchet. What do you say, dear boy?"

"Only too happy," said Severance, heartily. "And may we never unearth it again. Here comes Trent. He looks as if he had just been returned for the Senate."

"How are you?" demanded Trent, peremptorily. "You have made it up? Don't leave me out in the cold."

Dedham made a final lunge for his deserting dignity, then sent it on its way. "I should think not," he cried, with dancing eyes. "Give me your fist."

In a moment they were all shaking each other's hand off, and good-fellowship was streaming from every eye.

"Come over to my rooms, all of you," gurgled Teddy, "and have a drink."

"With pleasure, my boy," said Trent. "But native rudeness will compel me to drink and run. I am off for Newport—"

"Newport!" cried three voices.

"Yes; anything strange in that? I'm going on vital business connected with the coming election."

"This is a coincidence!" exclaimed Boswell, with the appreciation of the romanticist. "Why, we are all going to Newport. Dedham in search of health, Severance of pleasure, and I of a fortune—only the old mummy is always making out her cheques, but never passes them in. Well, I hope we'll see a lot of each other when we get there."

"Oh, of course," said Severance, hastily. "We will have many another game of polo together."

"Well," said Dedham, "come over to my rooms now and drink to the success of our separate quests."

III

Miss Decker paced restlessly up and down the sea-room waiting for the mail. Mrs. Pendleton, more composed but equally nervous, lay in a long chair, with expectation in her eyes and triumph on her lips.

"Will they answer or will they not?" exclaimed Miss Decker. "If the mail would only come! Will they be crushed?—furious?—or—will they apologise?"

"I care nothing what they do," said Mrs. Pendleton, languidly. "All I wanted was to see them when they received my notes, and later when they met to compare them. I hold that my revenge is a masterpiece—to turn the joke on them and to let them see that they could not make a fool of me at the same time! Oh! how dared they?"

"Well, they'll never perpetrate another practical joke, my dear. You have your revenge, Jessica; you have blunted their sense of humour for life. I doubt if they ever even read the funny page of a newspaper again. Here comes the postman. There! the bell has rung. Why doesn't Hart go? I'll go myself in a minute."

Mrs. Pendleton's nostrils dilated a little, but she did not turn her head even when the manservant entered and held a silver tray before her.

Four letters lay thereon. She placed them on her lap but did not speak until the man had left the room. Then she looked at Miss Decker and gave the letters a little sweep with the tips of her fingers.

"They have answered," she said.

"Oh, Jessica, for Heaven's sake don't be so iron-bound!" cried her friend. "Read them."

"You can read them if you choose. I have no interest beyond knowing that they received mine."

Miss Decker needed no second invitation. She caught the letters from Mrs. Pendleton's lap and tore one of them open. She read a few lines, then dropped limply on a chair.

"Jessica!" she whispered, with a little agonised gasp, "listen to this."

Mrs. Pendleton turned her eyes inquiringly, but would not stoop to curiosity. "Well," she said, "I am listening."

"It is from Mr. Trent. And—listen:—

"'Angel! I think if you had kept me waiting one day longer you would have met a lunatic wandering on the Newport cliffs. Last night I attended a primary and made such an egregious idiot of myself (although I was complimented later upon my speech) that I shall never understand why I was not hissed. But hereafter I shall be inspired. And how you will shine in Washington! That is the place for our talents. After reading your reserved yet impassioned note, I do not feel that I can talk more rationally upon politics than while in suspense. What do you think I did? I made it all up with Severance, Dedham, and Boswell, whom I met just after receiving it. I could afford to forgive them. They, by the way, go to Newport to-morrow. Farewell, most brilliant of women, destined by Heaven to be the wife of a diplomatist—for I will confide to you that that is my ultimate ambition. Until to-morrow,

"'Clarence Trent.'"

"Well! What do you think of that?"
A pink wave had risen to Mrs. Pendleton's hair, then receded and broken upon the haughty curve of her mouth.
"Read the others," she said briefly.
"Oh! how can you be so cool?" and Miss Decker opened another note with trembling fingers.
"It is from Norton Boswell:—

"'You once chided me for looking at the world through grey spectacles, and bade me always hope for the best until the worst was decided. When you were near to encourage me the sky was often pink, but even the memory of the last six months has faded before the agonised suspense of these seven days. Oh! I shall be an author now, if suffering is the final lesson. But what incoherent stuff I am writing! Loneliness and despair are alike forgotten. I can write no more! To-morrow! To-morrow!

"'Boswell.'"

"Read Severance's," said Jessica, quickly.
"I believe you like that man!" exclaimed Miss Decker. "I think he's a brute. But you're in a scrape. This is from the lordly Severance:—

"'An Englishman once said of you, with a drawl which wound the words about my memory—"Y-a-a-s; she flirts on ice, so to speak." Coldest and most subtle of women, why did you keep me in suspense for seven long days? Do you think I believe that fiction of the delayed letter? You forget that we have met before. But why torment me? Did I not in common decency have to wait six months before I dared put my fate to the test? How I counted those days! I had a calendar and a pencil—in short, I made a fool of myself. Now the chess-board is between us once more: we start on even ground; we will play a keen and close game to the end of our natural lives. I love you; but I know you. I will kiss the rod—

until we marry; after that—we shall play chess. I shall see you to-morrow.

"'S.'"

"Well, that's what I call a beast of a man," said Miss Decker.

"I hate him!" said Jessica, between her teeth.

She looked hard at the ocean. Under its grey sky to-day it was the colour of her eyes, as cold and as unfathomable. The glittering Medusa-like ends of her hair seemed to leap upward and writhe at each other.

"I should think you would hate him," said Miss Decker; "he is the only living man who ever got the best of you. But listen to what your devoted infant has to say. Nice little boy, Teddy:—

"'Dearest! Sweetest! Do you know that I am almost dancing for joy at this moment? Indeed, my feet are going faster than my pen. To think! To think!—you really *do* love me after all. But I always said you were not a flirt. I knocked a man down once and challenged him to a duel because he said you were. He wouldn't fight, but I had the satisfaction of letting him know what I thought of him. And now I can prove it to all the world! But I can't write any more. There are three blots on this now—the pen is jumping and you know I never was much at writing letters. But I can talk, and to-morrow I will tell you all.

"'Your own Teddy.

"'P.S.—Is it not queer—quite a coincidence—Severance, Trent, and Boswell are going to Newport to-morrow, too. How proud I shall be! But no, I take that back; I only pity them, poor devils, from the bottom of my heart; or I would if it wasn't filled up with you.

"'T.'"

"Well, madam, you're in a scrape, and I don't envy you. What will you do?" Mrs. Pendleton pressed her head against the back of the chair, straining her head upward as if she wanted the salt breeze to rasp her throat.

"I have been so bored for six months," she said slowly. "Let them come. I will see each of them alone, and keep the farce going for a week or so. It will be amusing—to be engaged to four men at once. You will command the forces and see that they do not meet. Of course, it cannot be kept up very long, and when all resources are failing I will let them meet and make them madly jealous. It will do one of them good, at least."

"Well, you have courage," ejaculated Miss Decker. "You can't do it. But yes, you can. If the woman lives who can play jackstraws with firebrands, that woman is you. And what fun! We are so dull here—both in mourning. I'll help you. I'll carry out your instructions like a major."

Mrs. Pendleton rose and walked up and down the room once or twice. "There is only one thing," she said, drawing her brows together: "if I am engaged to them they will want to—h'm—kiss me, you know. It will be rather awkward. I never was engaged to any one but Mr. Pendleton, and he used to kiss me on my forehead and say, 'My dear child.' I am afraid they won't be contented with that."

"I am afraid they won't! But you have tact enough. Come, say you will do it."

"Yes," said Jessica, "I will do it. In my boarding-school days I used to dream of being a tragedy queen; I find myself thrust by circumstances into comedy. But I have no doubt it will suit my talents better."

IV

SCENE I

Severance strode impatiently up and down the room overlooking the ocean. "'Will be down in a minute.' I suppose that means the usual thirty for reflection and contemplation of bric-à-brac. What a pretty room! No bric-à-brac in it, by the way. I wonder if this is the room my lady Jessica is said to have furnished to suit herself? It looks like a woodland glade. She must look stunning against those moss-green curtains. I wonder how madam liked my letter? It was rather brutal, but to manage a witch you have got to be Jove astride a high horse. Here she comes. I know that perfume. She uses it to sweeten the venom of those snakes of hers."

Mrs. Pendleton entered and gave him her hand with frank welcome. Her "snakes" seemed vibrant with life and defiance, and her individuality pierced through her white conventional gown like a solitary star in a hueless sky.

"How do you do?" she asked, shaking his hand warmly; then she sat down at once as a matter of course.

He understood the manœuvre.

"Let us play chess, by all means," he said and took a chair opposite. "Your seclusion has done you good," he added, smiling as the crest of a wave appeared in her eyes. "You have lost your fagged look and are more like a girl than a widow. Dissipation does not agree with you. Two more winters! You would try to make up for it by your wit, and then your nose would get sharp, and you would have a line down the middle of your forehead and another on each side of your mouth."

"You are as rude as ever," said Jessica, coldly; but the wave in her eyes threatened to become tidal. "If you marry a blonde and incarcerate her, however, you may find the effect more bleaching than Society."

"Was that a reflection upon my own society? I do not incarcerate; I only warn."

"So do I," said Mrs. Pendleton, significantly; "I have occasionally got the best of a bad bargain."

"And as you will find me the worst in the world you are already on the defensive," said Severance, with a laugh. "Come, I have not seen you for six months, and I am hard hit. I wrote you that I marked off each day with a pencil—a red one at that; I bought it for the occasion. Don't take a base advantage of the admission, but give me one kind syllable. I ask for it as humbly as a dog does for a bone."

"You do, indeed. I began by making disagreeable remarks about your personal appearance, did I not? If you will be a brute, I will be a—cat."

- 13 -

"You will acquit yourself with credit. But I will not quarrel with you to-day."
He rose suddenly and went over to her, but she was already on her feet. She dropped her eyes, then raised them appealingly; but the sea was level.
"Do not kiss me," she said.
"Why not?"
"I would rather not—yet. Do you know that I have never kissed a man—a lover, I mean—in my life? And this is so sudden—I would rather wait."
He raised her hand chivalrously to his lips. "I will wait," he said; "but you will wear my ring?" And he took a circlet from his pocket and slipped it on her finger.
"Thank you," she said simply and touched it with a little caressing motion.
He dropped her hand and stepped back. Miss Decker had pushed aside the portière.
"How do you do, Mr. Severance?" she said cordially; "I did not interrupt even to congratulate, but to take Jessica away for a moment. My dear, your dressmaker came down on the train with Mr. Severance and has but a minute. You had better go at once, for you know her temper is not sweet."
"Provoking thing!" said Jessica, with a pout. It was the fourth mood to which she treated Severance in this short interview, and he looked at her with delight. "But I will get rid of her as soon as possible. Will you excuse me for a few moments? I will be back in ten."
"A dressmaker is the only tyrant to whom I bow, the only foe before whom I lay down my arms. Go; but come back soon."
"In ten minutes."
"Which is it, and where is he?" she whispered eagerly as they crossed the hall.
"Mr. Trent. He is in the library."

SCENE II

Trent was standing before a bust of Daniel Webster, speculating upon how his own profile would look in bronze.
"You would have to shave off your side-whiskers," murmured a soft voice behind him.
He turned with a nervous start, and a suspicion of colour appeared under his grey skin. Mrs. Pendleton was standing with her hands resting lightly on the table. She smiled with saucy dignity—an art she had brought to perfection.
"I give you five years," she said.
"With you to help me," he cried enthusiastically. "Ah! I see you now, leaning on the arm of a foreign ambassador, going in to some great diplomatic dinner!"
"It is too bad, I shall have to take the arm of a small one; you will be but the American minister, you know. (Great Heaven! how determined he looks! I know he means to kiss me. If I can only keep his ambition going.)"

"I will be senator first, and pass a bill placing this country on an equal diplomatic footing with the proudest in Europe. You will then go to your embassy as the wife of an ambassador."

"I know you will accomplish it; and let it be Paris. I cannot endure to shop anywhere else."

"It shall be Paris."

"Are you not tired?" she asked hurriedly.

"Tired? I have not thought of fatigue."

"The day is so warm."

"I have not felt it. Jessica!"

"O—h—h—h!" and catching her face convulsively in her hand, she sank into a chair.

"What is it? What is it?" he cried, hopping about her like an agitated spider, the tip of his nose punctuating his excitement. "What can I do? Are you ill?"

Faintly: "Neuralgia."

"What shall I ring for? Antipyrine? Horse-radish for your wrists? Belladonna? What?"

"Nothing. Sit down and talk to me, and perhaps it will go away. Tell me something about yourself, and I'll forget it. Sit down."

"There is but little to tell. I have been busy making friends against the next election. I have addressed several meetings with great success. I have every chance for the House this time—for the Senate next term. How's your face?"

"Misery! You said that several of my old friends came down with you. How odd!"

"Was it not?"

"I suppose they will all come to see me."

"H'm. I don't know. Doubt if they know you are here. I shall not tell them. They would only be coming to see you and getting in my way. I'll wait until our wedding-day approaches and ask them to be ushers. But now, Jessica, that you do not seem to suffer so acutely—"

"Oh! Oh! (Thank Heaven, I hear Edith.)"

Trent sprang to his feet in genuine alarm. "Dearest! Let me go for the doctor. I cannot stand this—"

Miss Decker entered with apparent haste, spoke to Trent, then stopped abruptly.

"Jessica!" she cried. "What is the matter?"

"My face! You know how I have suffered—worse than ever."

"Oh, you poor dear! She is such a martyr, Mr. Trent, with that tooth—"

"Neuralgia!"

"I mean neuralgia! She was up all night. But, my dear, don't think me a heartless fiend, but you must see your lawyer. He is here with those deeds for you to sign, and he says that he must catch the train."

"That estate has given me so much trouble," murmured Mrs. Pendleton, wretchedly; "and how can I talk business when my head is on the rack? I do not wish to leave Mr. Trent so soon, either."

"Leave Mr. Trent to me. I will entertain him. I will talk to him about you."

"May I speak to you one moment before you go?" asked Trent.

"Yes," pinching her lips with extremest pain, "you need not mind Edith."

"Not in the least." He took a box from his pocket with an air of resignation which boded well for the trials of a diplomatic career. "I cannot wait longer to fetter you. You told me once that the emerald was your favourite stone." She relaxed her lips and swept her lashes down and up rapturously. "So good of you to remember," she murmured; "it reminds me of mermaids and things, and I love it."

"You were always so poetical! But where did you get that ring? I thought you never wore rings. On your engagement finger, too!"

"It was a present from grandma, and I wear it to please her. I'll slip it in my pocket now—it is too large for any other finger—and you can put yours where it belongs."

"You will never take it off until you need its place for your wedding-ring?"

"Never!"

"Angel! And your face is better?"

"Yes; but Edith is looking directly this way."

SCENE III

Mrs. Pendleton entered the drawing-room on tiptoe, with hand upraised.

"Well! the sky did not fall, and the train did not ditch, and the lightning did not strike, and we are neither of us dead. And you—you look as strapping as a West Point cadet. Fie upon your principles!"

"That is a charming tirade with which to greet an impatient lover," cried Boswell, with beaming face. "You are serious, of course?"

"You have heard the parable of a woman's 'No'?" She gave both his outstretched hands a little shake, then retreated behind a chair and rested both arms on its back.

"My anger is appeased, but I think I am entitled to some recompense."

"What can he mean? Would you prefer sherry or red wine?"

"There is a draught brewed upon Olympus which the gods call nectar—"

"So sorry. We are just out. I gave the last thimbleful away an hour ago."

"Oh, you did! May I inquire to whom you gave it?"

"You may, indeed. And I would tell you—could I only remember."

"Provoking—goddess! But perhaps you will allow me to look for myself. Perchance I might find a drop or two remaining. I am willing to take what I can get and be thankful."

"Then you will never get much," she thought. "The dregs are always bitter."

"There can be no dregs to the nectar in question."

"And the last drop always goes to the head. I have heard it asserted upon authority. Think of the scandal—the butler—oh, Heaven!"

"The intoxication would make me but tread the air. I should walk right over the butler's head. Where did you get that ring?"

"Is it not lovely? It was" (heaving a profound sigh) "the last gift of poor dear Mr. Pendleton."

"Indeed! Well, under the circumstances, perhaps you will not mind removing it and wearing that of another unfortunate," and he placed one knee on the chair over which she leaned and produced a ring.

"Not at all. What a beauty! How did you know that the ruby was my favourite stone?" And she bent her body backward, under pretence of holding the stone up to the light.

"But you have a number of rubies and pearls in your possession, of which I consider myself the rightful owner. Shall I have to call in the law to give me mine own?"

"The pearls are sharp, and the rubies may be paste. I have the best of the bargain."

"I am a connoisseur on the subject of precious stones—of precious articles of all sorts, in fact. What an outrageous coquette you are! What is the use of keeping a man in misery?"

"Why are men always in such a hurry? If I were a man now—and an author— I should wait for moonlight, waves breaking on rocks, and all the rest of it."

"All the old property business, in short. I am both a man and an author, therefore I know the folly of delay in this short life."

"But suppose the door should open suddenly?"

"I have been here ten minutes, and it has not opened yet."

"But it might, you know; and the small boys of this house are an exaggeration of all that have gone before. Ah! here comes some one. Sit down on that chair instantly."

Miss Decker entered and looked deprecatingly at Boswell.

"You have come at last," she said. "We were afraid something had happened to you. I cannot help this interruption, Jessica. Your grandmother is here and wants to see you immediately. She has been telegraphed for to go to Philadelphia; Mrs. Armstrong is very ill. I would not keep her waiting."

"Poor grandma! To think of her being obliged to go to Philadelphia in September. Where is she?"

"In the yellow reception-room. Mr. Boswell will excuse you for a few minutes."

Boswell bowed, his face stamped with gloom.

"What have you done with the others?" asked Jessica, as she closed the door.

"Mr. Severance is storming up and down the sea-room. Mr. Trent is like a caged lion in the library; I expect to hear a crash every minute. But both know what lawyers and dressmakers mean. Boswell will learn something of grandmothers. But they are safe for a quarter of an hour longer. Trust all to me."

SCENE IV

Dedham was sitting on the edge of one of the reception-room chairs, locking and unlocking his fingers until his hands were as red as those of a son of toil. He was nervous, happy, terrified, annoyed.

"That beastly porter to keep me waiting so long for my portmanteau!" he almost cried aloud. "What must she think of me?"

"You wicked boy!" said a voice of gentle reproach. "What made you so late? I was just about to send and inquire if anything had happened to you. But sit down. How tired you must be! Would you like a glass of sherry and a biscuit?"

"Nothing! Nothing! You know, it's not my fault that I'm late. My portmanteau got mislaid and my travelling clothes were so dusty. And you really are glad to see me?"

"What a question! It makes me feel young again to see you."

"Young again! You!"

"I am twenty-four, Teddy, and a widow," and she shook her head sadly. "I feel fearfully old—like your mother. I have had so much care and responsibility in my life, and you are so careless and debonair."

"You'll make me cry in a minute," said Teddy; "and I wish you wouldn't talk like that. You seem to put a whole Adirondack between us."

"I can't help it. Perhaps I'll get over it after a time. It's so sad being mewed up six whole months!"

"Then marry me right off. That's just the point. We'll go and travel and have a jolly good time. That'll brace you up and make you feel as young as you look."

"I can't, Teddy. I must wait a year in common decency. Think how people would talk."

"Let 'em. They'll soon find something else and forget us. Marry me next month."

"Next month—well—"

"It would be rather fun to be the hero and heroine of a sensation, anyhow. That's what everybody's after. You're just a nonentity until you've been black-guarded in the papers. Whose ring is that?"

"One of Edith's. I put it on to remember something by."

"Well, take it off and wear this instead. It'll help your memory just as well."

"What, a solitaire!"

"I knew you would prefer it. I know all your tastes by instinct."

"You do, Teddy. Coloured stones are so tiresome."

"By the way, I think your old admirer, Severance, must be about to put himself in silken fetters, as Boswell would say. I caught him buying an

- 18 -

unusually fine sapphire in Tiffany's yesterday. Said it was for his sister. H'm—h'm."

"Ah! I wonder who it can be?"

"Don't know. Hasn't looked at a woman since you left. But I have a strong suspicion that it is some one here in Newport."

"Here! I wonder if it can be Edith?"

"Miss Decker? Sure enough. Never seemed to pay her much attention, though. She's not my style; too much like sixteen dozen other New York girls."

He buttoned up his coat, braced himself against it, and gave his moustache a frantic twist.

"Mrs.—Jessica!" he ejaculated desperately, "you are engaged to me—won't you—won't you—"

She drew herself up and glanced down upon him from her higher chair with a look of sad disapproval.

"I did not think it of you, Teddy," she said. "And it is one of the things of which I have never approved."

"But why not?" asked Teddy, feebly.

"I thought you knew me better than to ask such a question."

"I know you are an angel—oh, hang it! You do make me feel as if you *were* my mother."

"Now, don't be unreasonable, or I shall believe that you are a tyrant."

"A tyrant? I? Horri—no, I wish I was. What a model of propriety you are! I never should have thought it—I mean—darling! you were always such a coquette, you know. Not that I ever thought so. You know I never did—oh, hang it all—but if I let you have your own way in this unreasonable—I mean this perfectly natural whim—you might at least promise to marry me in a month. And, indeed, I think that if you are an angel, I am a saint."

"Well, on one condition."

"Any! Any!"

"It must be an absolute secret until the wedding is over. I hate congratulations, and if we are going to have a sensation we might as well have a good concentrated one."

"I agree with you, and I'll never find fault with you again. You—"

Miss Decker almost ran into the room.

"Jessica!" she cried. "Oh, dear Mr. Dedham, how are you? Jessica, mother has one of her terrible attacks, and I must ask you to stay with her while I go for the doctor myself. I cannot trust servants."

"Let me go! let me go!" cried Teddy. "I'll bring him back in a quarter of an hour. Who shall—"

"Coleman. He lives—"

"I know. Au revoir!" And the girls were alone.

"There!" exclaimed Miss Decker, "we have got rid of him. Now for the others. You slip upstairs, and I'll dispose of them one by one. You are taken suddenly ill. Teddy will not be back for an hour. Dr. Coleman has moved."

V

A lamp burned in the sea-room, and the two girls were sitting in their evening gowns before a bright log fire. Miss Decker was in white this time—an elaborate French concoction of embroidered muslin which made her look like an expensive fashion plate. Jessica wore a low-cut black crêpe, above which she rose like carved ivory and brass. The snakes to-night were held in place by diamond hair-pins that glittered like baleful eyes. In her lap sparkled four rings.

"What shall I do?" she exclaimed. "If my life depended upon it, I could not remember who gave me which."

"Let us think. What sort of a stone would a politician be most likely to choose?"

Mrs. Pendleton laughed. "A good idea. If couleur de rose be synonymous with conceit, then I think the ruby must have come from Mr. Trent."

"I am sure of it. And as your author is always in the dumps, I am certain he takes naturally to the sapphire."

"But the emerald—"

"Is emblematic of your deluded Teddy. The solitaire therefore falls naturally to Mr. Severance. Well, now that you have got through the first interviews in safety, what are you going to do next?"

"Edith, I do not know. They are all so dreadfully in earnest that I believe I shall finally take to my heels in down-right terror. But no, I won't. I'll come out of it with the upper hand and save my reputation as an actress. I will keep it up for two or three days more, but after that it will be impossible. They are bound to meet here sooner or later. Thank Heaven, we are rid of them for to-night, at least!"

The manservant threw back the portière.

"Mr. Trent!"

"Heavens!" cried Edith, under her breath; "I forgot to give orders that we were not receiv—how do you do, Mr. Trent?"

"And which is his ring?" Jessica made a frenzied dab at the jewels in her lap. She slipped the sapphire on her finger and hid the others under a cushion. Trent, who had been detained a moment by Miss Decker, advanced to her.

"It is very soon to come again," he said, "but I simply had to call and inquire if you felt better. I am delighted to see that you apparently do."

"I am better, thank you." Her voice was weak. "It was good of you to come again."

"Whose ring is that?"

"Why—a—to—sure—"

"Jessica!" cried Miss Decker, "have you gone off with my ring again? You are so absent-minded! I hunted for that ring high and low!"

"You should not be so good-natured, and my memory would turn over a new leaf. Here, take it." She tossed the ring to Miss Decker and raised her eyes guiltily to Trent's. "Shall I go up and get the other?"

"No. But I thought you promised never to take it off."

"I forgot that water ruins stones."

"Well, it is a consolation to know that water does not ruin a certain plain gold circlet."

"Mr. Boswell!"

Jessica gasped and looked at the flames. A crisis had come. Would she be clever enough? Then the situation stimulated her. She held out her hand to Boswell.

"You have come to see me?" she cried delightedly. "Mr. Trent has just been telling us that you came down with him, and I hoped you would call soon."

"Yes, to be sure—to be sure. You might have known I would call soon." He bowed stiffly to Trent, and, seating himself close beside Jessica, murmured in her ear: "Cannot you get rid of that fellow? How did he find you out so soon?"

"Why, he came to see Edith, of course. Do you not remember how devoted he always was to her?"

"I do not—"

"May I ask what you are whispering about, Mr. Boswell?" demanded Trent, breaking from Miss Decker. "Is he confiding to you the astounding success of his last novel, Mrs. Pendleton? Or was it a history of the United States? I really forget."

"Not the last, certainly. I leave it to you to make history—an abridged edition. My ambition is a more humble one."

"Oh, you will both need biographers," said Mrs. Pendleton, who was beginning to enjoy herself. "I will give you an idea. Join the Theosophists. Arrange for reincarnation. Come back in the next generation and write your own biographies. Then your friends and families cannot complain you have not had justice done you."

"Ha! ha!" said Trent.

"You are as cruel as ever," said Boswell, with a sigh. "Where is my ring?" he whispered.

"It was so large that I could not keep it on. I must have a guard made."

"Dear little fingers—"

"You may never have been taught when you were a small boy, Mr. Boswell," interrupted Trent, "that it is rude to whisper in company. Therefore, to save your manners in Mrs. Pendleton's eyes, I will do you the kindness to prevent further lapse." And he seated himself on the other side of Jessica and glared defiantly at Boswell.

"Mr. Severance and Mr. Dedham!"

Severance entered hurriedly. "I am so glad to hear—ah, Boswell! Trent!"

"How odd that you should all find your way here the very first evening of your arrival!" And Jessica held out her hand with a placid smile. Miss Decker was more nervous, but five seasons were behind her. "Ah!" continued Mrs. Pendleton, "and Mr. Dedham, too! This is a most charming reunion!"

"Charming beyond expression!" said Severance.

Trent and Boswell being obliged to rise when Miss Decker went forward to meet the newcomers, Severance took the former's chair, Dedham that of the future statesman.

"You are better?" whispered Severance. "I have been anxious."

"Oh, I have been worried to death!" murmured Teddy in her other ear. "That wretched doctor had not only moved but gone out of town; and when I came back at last and found—"

"Mr. Severance," exclaimed Trent, "you have my chair."

"Is this your chair? You have good taste. A remarkably comfortable chair."

"You would oblige me—"

"By keeping it? Certainly. You were ever generous, but that I believe is a characteristic of genius."

"Mrs. Pendleton," said Boswell, plaintively, "as Mr. Dedham has taken my chair, I will take this stool at your feet."

Trent was obliged to lean his elbow on the mantelpiece, for want of a better view of Mrs. Pendleton, and Miss Decker sat on the other side of Dedham.

"How are you, Teddy?" she said.

"Young and happy. You must let me congratulate you."

"For what?"

"I see you wear Severance's ring. Ah, Sev, did the ring suit your sister?"

"To a T. Said it was her favourite stone." He stopped abruptly. "What the deuce—" below his breath; and Jessica whispered hurriedly:—

"Edith was looking at it when Mr. Trent came in, and forgot to return it."

"Ah! Boswell, I am sure you are sitting on Mrs. Pendleton's foot. By the way, how is your aunt?"

"Dead—better."

"I wonder you could tear yourself away so soon," said Trent, viciously. "You'd better be careful. She might make a new will."

"Don't worry. I spent the happiest fifteen minutes of my life with her this afternoon. She promised me all." He turned to Severance. "You have been breaking hearts on the beach, I suppose."

"Which is better, at all events, than breaking one's head against a stone wall."

"Politics brought you here, I suppose, Mr. Trent," interrupted Miss Decker. "I hear you made a stirring speech the other night."

"I did. It was on the question of Radicalism in the Press *versus* Civil Service Reform. Something must be done to revolutionise this hotbed of iniquity, American politics. Such principles need courage, but when the hour comes the man must not be wanting—"

"That was all in the paper next morning," drawled Boswell. "Mrs. Pendleton, did you receive the copy of my new book I sent a fortnight ago? Unlike many of my others, I had no difficulty in disposing of it. It was lighter, brighter, less philosophy, less—brains. The critics understood it, therefore they were kind. They even said—"

"Don't quote the critics, for Heaven's sake," said Severance. "It is enough to have read them."

"Oh, Mrs. Pendleton," exclaimed Teddy, "if you could have been at the yacht race! Such excitement, such—"

"To change the subject," said Trent, with determination in his eye, "Mrs. Pendleton, did you receive all the marked papers I sent you containing my speeches, especially the one on Jesuitism in Politics?"

"Don't bother Mrs. Pendleton with politics!" exclaimed Boswell, whose own egotism was kicking against its bars. "You did not think my book too long, did you? One purblind critic said—"

"Good night, Mrs. Pendleton," said Severance, rising abruptly. "Good evening," and he bowed to Miss Decker and to the men. Jessica rose suddenly and went with him to the door.

"I am going to walk on the cliffs—'Forty Steps'—at eleven to-morrow," she said, as she gave him her hand. "This may be unconventional, but *I* choose to do it."

He bowed over her hand. "Mrs. Pendleton will only have set one more fashion," he said. "I shall be there."

As he left the room by one door, Jessica crossed the room and opened another.

"Good night," she said to the astounded company, and withdrew.

VI

Severance sauntered up and down the "Forty Steps," the repose of his bearing belying the agitation within.

"Why on earth doesn't she come?" he thought uneasily. "Can she be ill again? She is ten minutes behind time now. What did it mean—all those fellows there last night? She looked like an amused spectator at a play, and Miss Decker was nervous, actually nervous. Damn it! Here they all come. What do they mean by keeping under my heels like this?"

Dedham, Trent, and Boswell strolled up from various directions, and, although each had expectation in his eye, none looked overjoyed to see the other men. There were four cold nods, a dead pause, and then Teddy gave a little cough.

"Beautiful after—I mean morning."

"It is indeed," said Severance. "I wonder you are not taking your salt-water constitutional."

"I always take a walk in the morning;" and Teddy glanced nervously over his shoulder.

Boswell and Trent, each with a little missive burning his pocket, turned red, fidgeted, glared at the ocean, and made no remark. Severance darted a glance at each of the three in succession, and then looked at the ground with a contemplative stare. At this moment Mrs. Pendleton appeared.

Three of the men advanced to meet her with an awkward attempt at surprise, but she waved them back.

"I have something to say to you," she said.

The cold languor of her face had given place to an expression of haughty triumph. A gleam of conscious power lay deep in her scornful eyes. The final act in the drama had come, and the dénouement should be worthy of her talents. She looked like a judge who had smiled encouragement to a guilty defendant only to confer the sentence of capital punishment at last.

"Gentlemen," she said, and even her voice was judicatorial, "I have asked you all to meet me here this morning"—(three angry starts, but she went on unmoved)—"because I came to the conclusion last night that it is quite time this farce should end. I am somewhat bored myself, and I have no doubt you are so, as well. Your joke was a clever one, worthy of the idle days of autumn. When I received your four proposals by the same mail, I appreciated your wit—I will say more, your genius—and felt glad to do anything I could to contribute to your amusement, especially as all the world is away and I knew how dull you must be. So I accepted each of you, as you know, had four charming interviews and one memorable one of a more composite nature; and now that we have all agreed that the spicy and original little drama has run its length I take pleasure in restoring your rings."

She took from her handkerchief a beautiful little casket of blue onyx, upon which reposed the Pendleton crest in diamonds, touched a spring, and revealed four rings sparkling about as many velvet cushions. The four men stood speechless; not one dared protest his sincerity and see ridicule in the eyes of his neighbour.

Mrs. Pendleton dropped her judicial air, and taking the ruby between her fingers, smiled like a teacher bestowing a prize.

"Mr. Boswell," she said, "I believe this belongs to you;" and she handed the ring to the stupefied author. He put it in his pocket with never a word.

She raised the emerald. "Mr. Trent, this is yours?—or is it the sapphire?"

"'WELL, WHY DON'T YOU GO?'"

"The emerald," snorted Trent.

She dropped it in his nerveless palm with a gracious bend of the head, and turned to Teddy.

"You gave me a solitaire, I remember," she said sweetly. "A most appropriate gift, for it is the ideal life."

Teddy looked as if about to burst into tears, gave her one beseeching glance, then took his ring and strode feebly over the cliffs. Trent and Boswell hesitated a moment, then hurried after.

Jessica held the casket to Severance, with a little outward sweep of her wrist. He took it and, folding his arms, looked at her steadily. A tide of angry colour rose to her hair, then she turned her back upon him and looking out over the water tapped her foot on the rocks.

"Why do you not go?" she asked. "I hate you more than any one on earth."

"No. You love me."

"I hate you! You are a brute! The coolest, the rudest, the most exasperating man on—on earth."

"That is the reason you love me. My dear Mrs. Pendleton," he continued, taking the ring from the casket and laying the latter on a rock, "a woman of brains and headstrong will—but unegoistic—likes a brutal and masterful man. An egoistical woman, whether she be fool or brilliant, likes a slave. The reason is that egoism, not being a feminine quality primarily, but borrowed from man, places its fair possessor outside of her sex's limitations and supplies her with the satisfying simulacrum of those stronger characteristics which she would otherwise look for in man. You are not an egoist."

He took her hand and removed her glove in spite of her resistance.

"Don't struggle. You would only look ridiculous if any one should pass. Besides, it is useless. I am so much stronger. I do not know or care what really possessed you to indulge in such a freak as to engage yourself to four men at once," he continued, slipping the ring on her finger. "You had your joke, and I hope you enjoyed it. The dénouement was highly dramatic. As I said, I desire no explanation, for I am never concerned with anything but results. And now—you are going to marry me."

"I am not!" sobbed Jessica.

"You are." He glanced about. No one was in sight. He put his arm about her shoulders, forcing her own to her sides, then bent back her head and kissed her on the mouth.

"Checkmate!" he said.

GERTRUDE ATHERTON was born in San Francisco and received her early education in California and Kentucky, but her best training was in her grandfather's library, a collection, it is said, of English masterpieces only, containing no American fiction whatever. Yet Mrs. Atherton is as thorough an American as a niece, in the third generation, of Benjamin Franklin should be.

It seems to have been the English critics who first recognised her originality, power, intensity, vividness, and vitality, but from her first book, "What Dreams May Come," published in 1888, her writings have revealed the unusual combination of brains and feeling. This gives her work both keen, clever strength and brilliancy of colour, developed through years of hard work, many of which were spent abroad, and reaching their best manifestation in her latest fiction, the one quality in "The Conqueror" and the other in "The Splendid Idle Forties." Both of these books go to prove the foresight of Mr. Harold Frederic, who, shortly before his death, declared her to be "the only woman in contemporary literature who knew how to write a novel," and that her future work would be her best. Another eminent English critic, Dr. Robertson Nicholl, spoke for some of the best students of modern literature in saying:—

"Gertrude Atherton is the ablest woman writer of fiction now living."

In her most notable novel, "The Conqueror," Gertrude Atherton has chosen in "the true and romantic story of Alexander Hamilton" a subject which would have attracted few woman writers, and has handled those parts of it with which many men have busied their brains in such a way that *The New York Times Saturday Review* remarked that it

"Holds more romance than nine-tenths of the imaginative fiction of the day and more veracity than ninety-nine hundredths of the history. She is master of her material."

"Certainly this country has produced no writer who approaches Mrs. Atherton," says one critic, while another adds that to have so "re-created a great man as Mrs. Atherton has done in this novel is to have written one's own title to greatness." All alike regard it as "a thing apart" (*The Critic*); "a remarkable production, full of force, vigour, brains, and insight" (*Boston Herald*); "an entrancing book ... brilliantly written" (*Glasgow Herald*). "It is hardly too much to say that she has invented a new kind of historical novel" is the comment of the *Athenæum* (London), with the addition that "the experiment is a remarkable success."

Equally strong in fascination and vigour is "The Splendid Idle Forties," but as far removed from "The Conqueror" as were the

Eastern and Western seaboards of this country in the times of which the stories treat, "the long, drowsy, shimmering days before the Gringo came," to the California of which she writes. "Pointed, spirited, and Spanish" are these "rich and impressive" stories; "such as could hardly have been told in any other country since the Bagdad of the 'Thousand and One Nights.' The book is full of weird fascination, and will add to Mrs. Atherton's deservedly high reputation," says *The Athenæum*.

> "In this book even more than in her others is shown that imaginative brilliancy so striking as to set one wondering what is the secret of the effect. . . . For the rest, her charm lies in temperament, magnetic, restless, assertive, vivid."—*Washington Times*.

In close relation to "The Conqueror" stands Mrs. Atherton's still more recent selection of "A Few of Hamilton's Letters," chosen from the great bulk of his state papers and other letters in such a way as to bring to the average reader the means of estimating the personality of this remarkable man from his own words. Incidentally it is the surest refutation of some of the hasty criticisms upon the picture of him in "The Conqueror," where, as Mr. Le Gallienne justly observes, "it was reserved for Mrs. Atherton to make him really alive to the present generation."

Milton Keynes UK
Ingram Content Group UK Ltd.
UKHW050924170424
441314UK00004B/207

9 789357 954853